D0842379

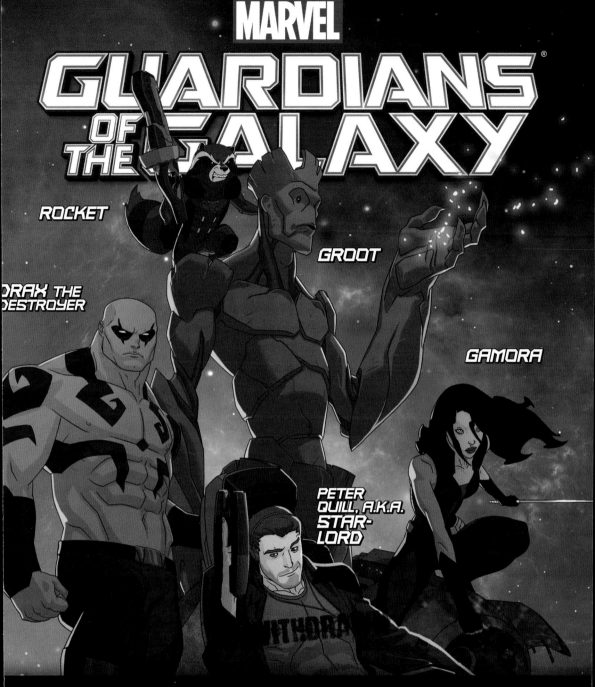

MARVEL
GUARDIANS OF THE GALAXY®

ROCKET

GROOT

DRAX THE DESTROYER

GAMORA

PETER QUILL, A.K.A. STAR-LORD

PREVIOUSLY:

The Guardians came into possession of a mysterious Spartaxan cube that they learned once held an object of immense power called the Cosmic Seed. Half-Spartaxan, Star-Lord was able to open the box to discover it contains a partial map to the Seed. The Guardians are now protecting the cube, but need a Pandorian crystal to fully unlock the map and track down the Cosmic Seed...

Volume 4: Take the *Milano* and Run
BASED ON THE DISNEY XD ANIMATED TV SERIES

Written by ANDREW R. ROBINSON   Directed by JEFF WAMESTER
Animation Art Produced by MARVEL ANIMATION STUDIOS   Adapted by JOE CARAMAGNA

Special Thanks to
HANNAH MACDONALD
& PRODUCT FACTORY

MARK BASSO editor
AXEL ALONSO editor in chief
DAN BUCKLEY publisher

MARK PANICCIA senior editor
JOE QUESADA chief creative officer
ALAN FINE executive producer

ABDOPUBLISHING.COM

Reinforced library bound edition published in 2018 by Spotlight,
a division of ABDO, PO Box 398166, Minneapolis, Minnesota 55439.
Spotlight produces high-quality reinforced library bound editions for
schools and libraries. Published by agreement with Marvel Characters, Inc.

Printed in the United States of America, North Mankato, Minnesota.
042017
092017

marvelkids.com
© 2017 MARVEL

PUBLISHER'S CATALOGING IN PUBLICATION DATA

Names: Robinson, Andrew R. ; Caramagna, Joe, authors. | Marvel Animation,
   illustrator.
Title: Take the Milano and run / writers: Andrew R. Robinson ; Joe Caramagna ; art:
   Marvel Animation.
Description: Reinforced library bound edition. | Minneapolis, Minnesota : Spotlight,
   2018. | Series: Guardians of the galaxy ; volume 4
Summary: After crash landing on a space station called Conjunction, the Guardians
   search for Pandorian Crystals while avoiding fighting in the Conjunction Arena
   and being busted by Nova Corpsman Titus.
Identifiers: LCCN 2017931209 | ISBN 9781532140730 (lib. bdg.)
Subjects: LCSH: Superheroes--Juvenile fiction. | Adventure and adventurers--
   Juvenile fiction. | Comic books, strips, etc.--Juvenile fiction. | Graphic novels--
   Juvenile fiction.
Classification: DDC 741.5--dc23
LC record available at https://lccn.loc.gov/2017931209

Spotlight

A Division of ABDO
abdopublishing.com

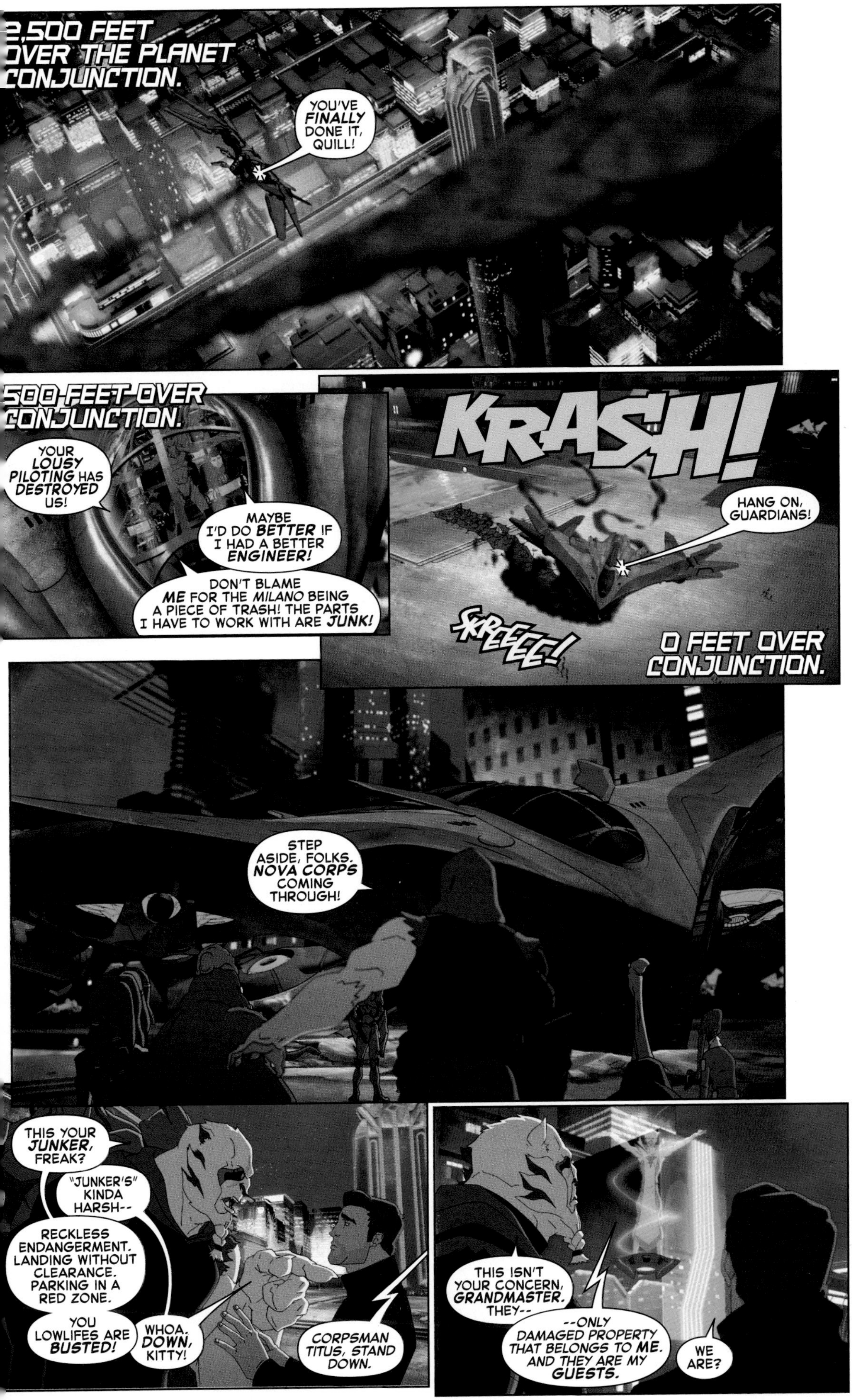

2,500 FEET OVER THE PLANET CONJUNCTION.
YOU'VE FINALLY DONE IT, QUILL!
500 FEET OVER CONJUNCTION.
YOUR LOUSY PILOTING HAS DESTROYED US!
MAYBE I'D DO BETTER IF I HAD A BETTER ENGINEER!
DON'T BLAME ME FOR THE MILANO BEING A PIECE OF TRASH! THE PARTS I HAVE TO WORK WITH ARE JUNK!
KRASH!
HANG ON, GUARDIANS!
SKREEEEE!
0 FEET OVER CONJUNCTION.
STEP ASIDE, FOLKS. NOVA CORPS COMING THROUGH!
THIS YOUR JUNKER, FREAK?
"JUNKER'S" KINDA HARSH--
RECKLESS ENDANGERMENT. LANDING WITHOUT CLEARANCE. PARKING IN A RED ZONE.
YOU LOWLIFES ARE BUSTED!
WHOA. DOWN, KITTY!
CORPSMAN TITUS, STAND DOWN.
THIS ISN'T YOUR CONCERN, GRANDMASTER. THEY--
--ONLY DAMAGED PROPERTY THAT BELONGS TO ME. AND THEY ARE MY GUESTS.
WE ARE?

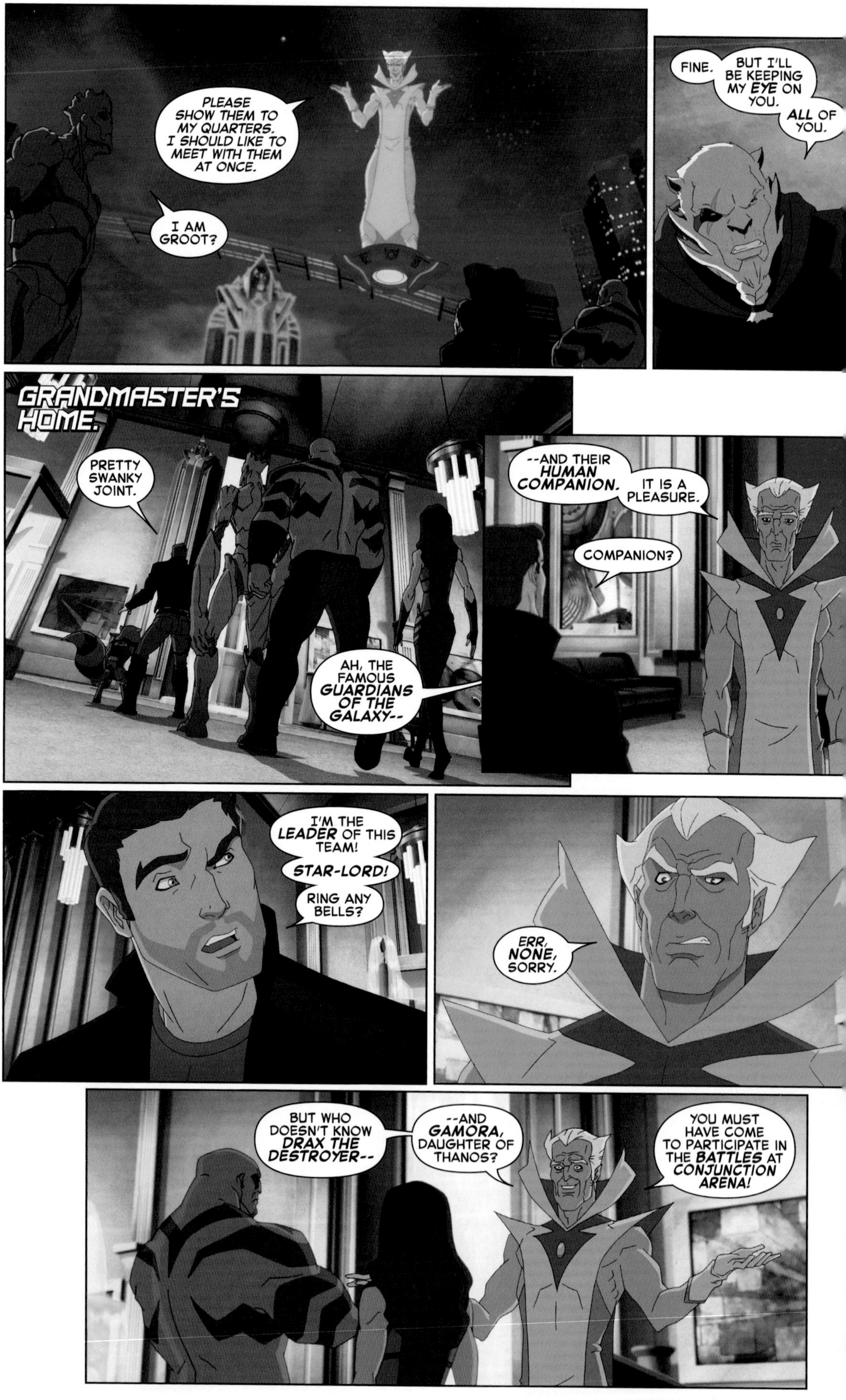
PLEASE SHOW THEM TO MY QUARTERS. I SHOULD LIKE TO MEET WITH THEM AT ONCE.
I AM GROOT?
FINE.
BUT I'LL BE KEEPING MY EYE ON YOU.
ALL OF YOU.
GRANDMASTER'S HOME.
PRETTY SWANKY JOINT.
AH, THE FAMOUS GUARDIANS OF THE GALAXY--
--AND THEIR HUMAN COMPANION.
IT IS A PLEASURE.
COMPANION?
I'M THE LEADER OF THIS TEAM!
STAR-LORD!
RING ANY BELLS?
ERR, NONE, SORRY.
BUT WHO DOESN'T KNOW DRAX THE DESTROYER--
--AND GAMORA, DAUGHTER OF THANOS?
YOU MUST HAVE COME TO PARTICIPATE IN THE BATTLES AT CONJUNCTION ARENA!

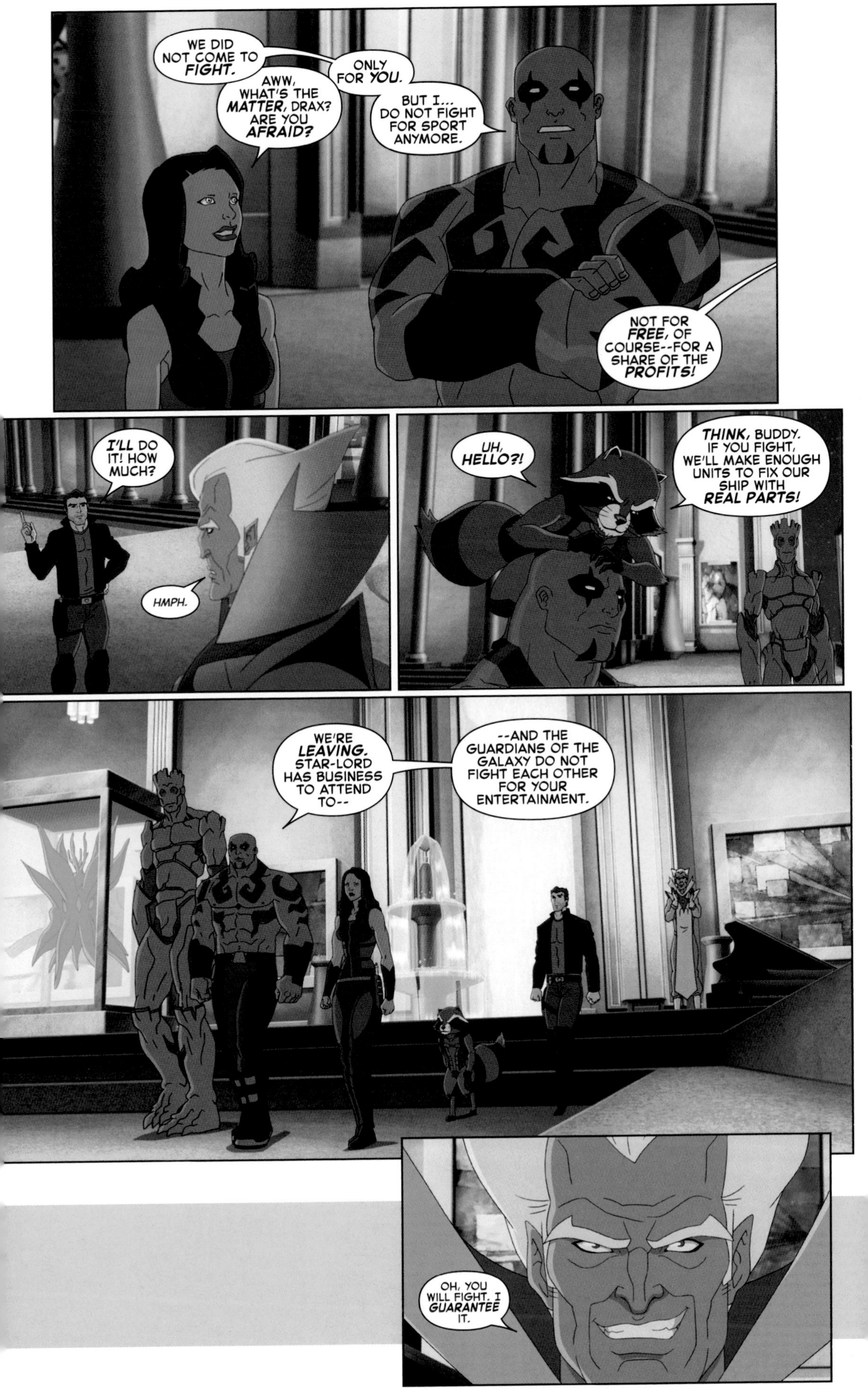
WE DID NOT COME TO FIGHT.
AWW, WHAT'S THE MATTER, DRAX? ARE YOU AFRAID?
ONLY FOR YOU.
BUT I... DO NOT FIGHT FOR SPORT ANYMORE.
NOT FOR FREE, OF COURSE--FOR A SHARE OF THE PROFITS!
I'LL DO IT! HOW MUCH?
HMPH.
UH, HELLO?!
THINK, BUDDY. IF YOU FIGHT, WE'LL MAKE ENOUGH UNITS TO FIX OUR SHIP WITH REAL PARTS!
WE'RE LEAVING. STAR-LORD HAS BUSINESS TO ATTEND TO--
--AND THE GUARDIANS OF THE GALAXY DO NOT FIGHT EACH OTHER FOR YOUR ENTERTAINMENT.
OH, YOU WILL FIGHT. I GUARANTEE IT.

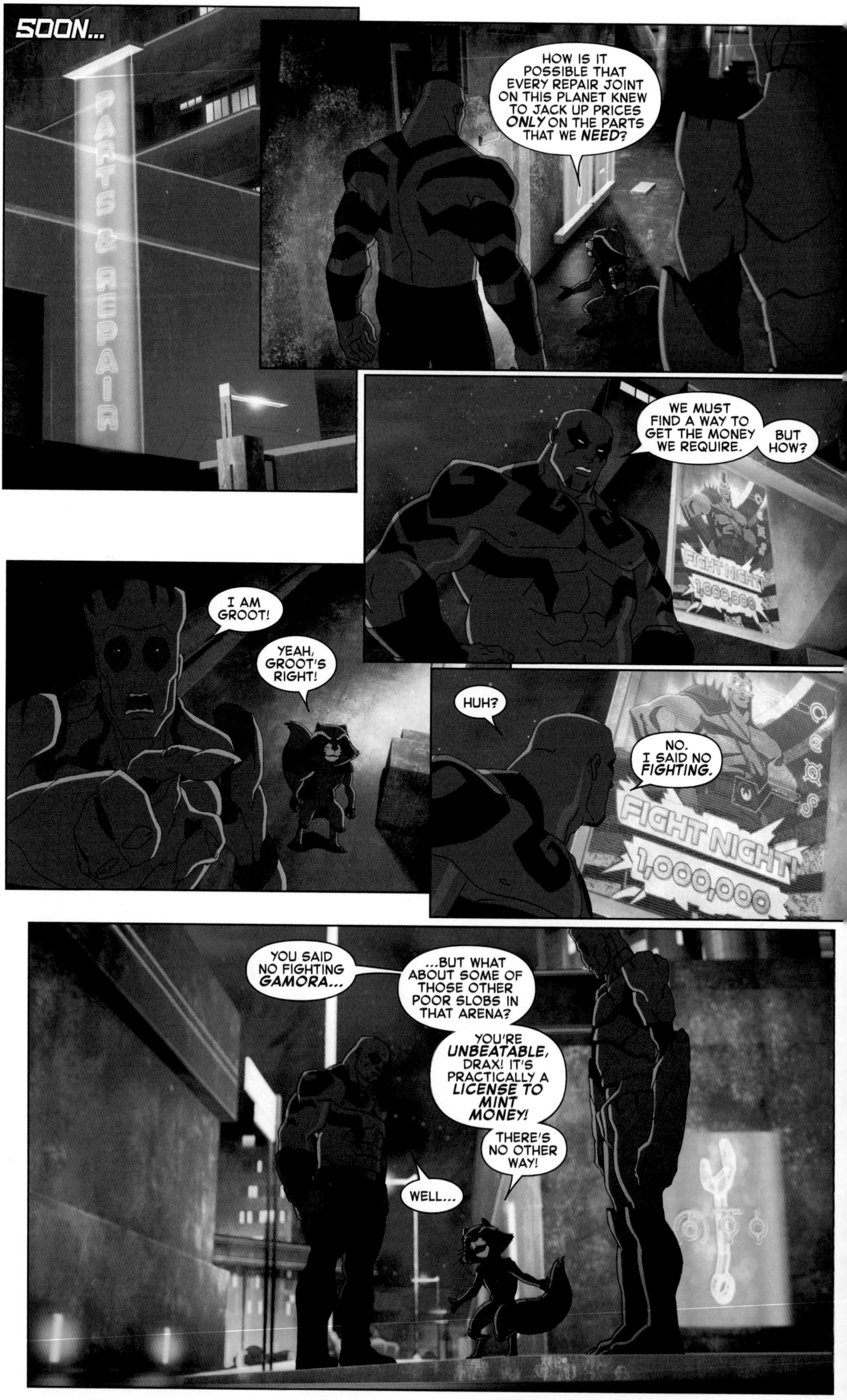
SOON...
PARTS & REPAIR
HOW IS IT POSSIBLE THAT EVERY REPAIR JOINT ON THIS PLANET KNEW TO JACK UP PRICES ONLY ON THE PARTS THAT WE NEED?
WE MUST FIND A WAY TO GET THE MONEY WE REQUIRE.
BUT HOW?
FIGHT NIGHT
1,000,000
I AM GROOT!
YEAH, GROOT'S RIGHT!
HUH?
NO. I SAID NO FIGHTING.
FIGHT NIGHT
1,000,000
YOU SAID NO FIGHTING GAMORA...
...BUT WHAT ABOUT SOME OF THOSE OTHER POOR SLOBS IN THAT ARENA?
YOU'RE UNBEATABLE, DRAX! IT'S PRACTICALLY A LICENSE TO MINT MONEY!
THERE'S NO OTHER WAY!
WELL...

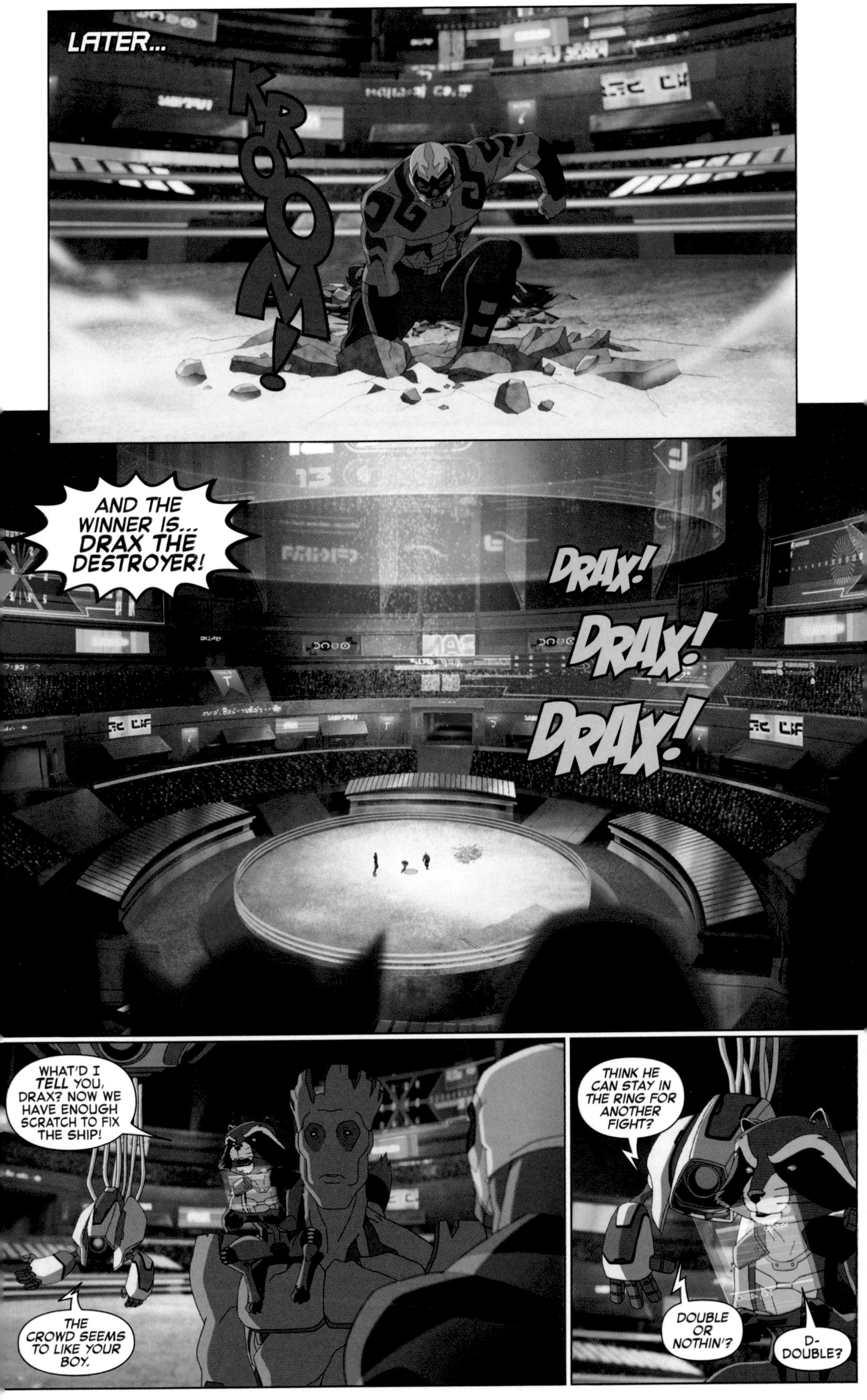
LATER...
KROOM!
AND THE WINNER IS... DRAX THE DESTROYER!
DRAX! DRAX! DRAX!
WHAT'D I TELL YOU, DRAX? NOW WE HAVE ENOUGH SCRATCH TO FIX THE SHIP!
THE CROWD SEEMS TO LIKE YOUR BOY.
THINK HE CAN STAY IN THE RING FOR ANOTHER FIGHT?
DOUBLE OR NOTHIN'?
D-DOUBLE?

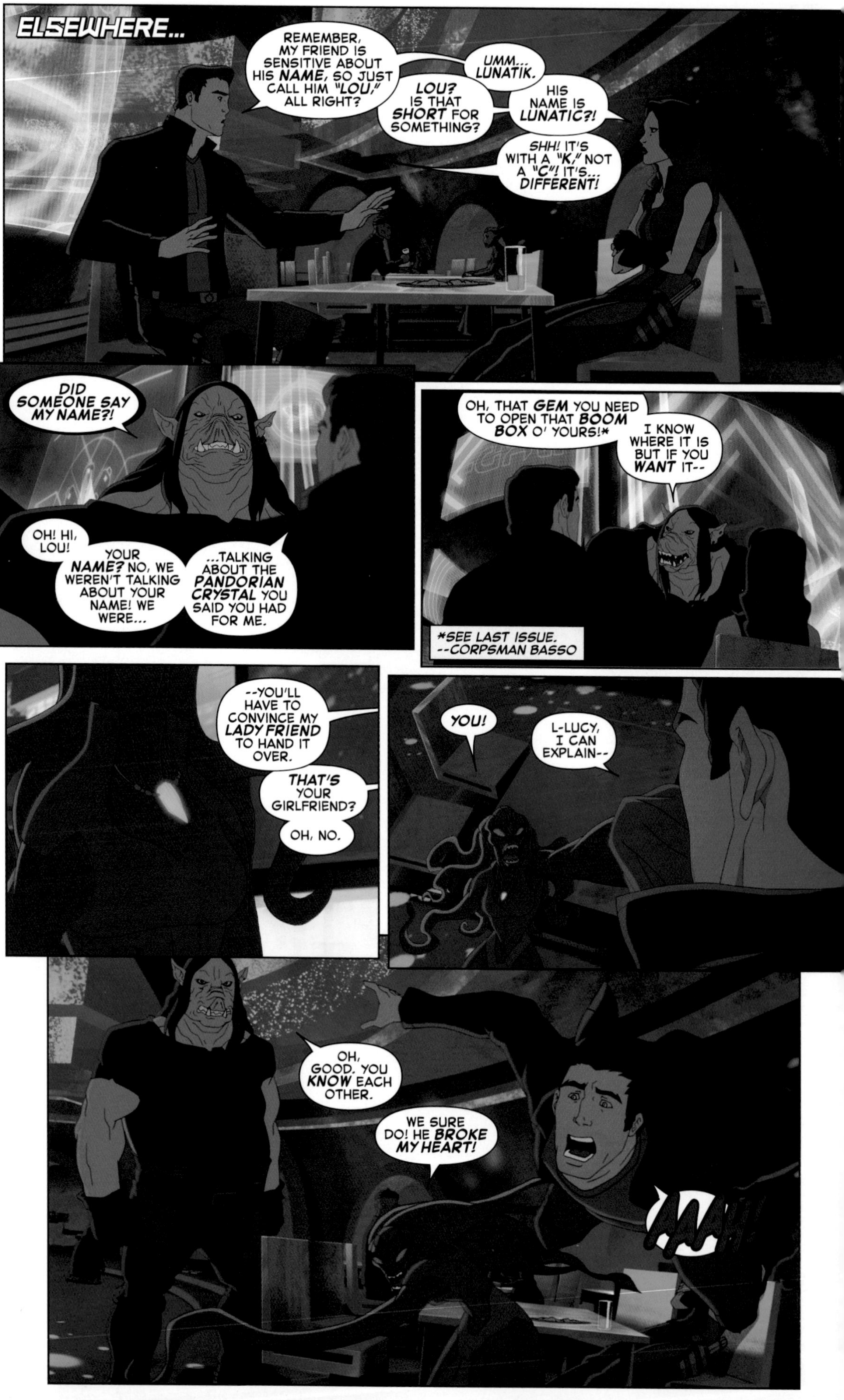
ELSEWHERE...
REMEMBER, MY FRIEND IS SENSITIVE ABOUT HIS NAME, SO JUST CALL HIM "LOU," ALL RIGHT?
LOU? IS THAT SHORT FOR SOMETHING?
UMM... LUNATIK.
HIS NAME IS LUNATIC?!
SHH! IT'S WITH A "K," NOT A "C"! IT'S... DIFFERENT!
DID SOMEONE SAY MY NAME?!
OH! HI, LOU!
YOUR NAME? NO, WE WEREN'T TALKING ABOUT YOUR NAME! WE WERE...
...TALKING ABOUT THE PANDORIAN CRYSTAL YOU SAID YOU HAD FOR ME.
OH, THAT GEM YOU NEED TO OPEN THAT BOOM BOX O' YOURS!*
I KNOW WHERE IT IS BUT IF YOU WANT IT--
*SEE LAST ISSUE. --CORPSMAN BASSO
--YOU'LL HAVE TO CONVINCE MY LADY FRIEND TO HAND IT OVER.
THAT'S YOUR GIRLFRIEND?
OH, NO.
YOU!
L-LUCY, I CAN EXPLAIN--
OH, GOOD. YOU KNOW EACH OTHER.
WE SURE DO! HE BROKE MY HEART!

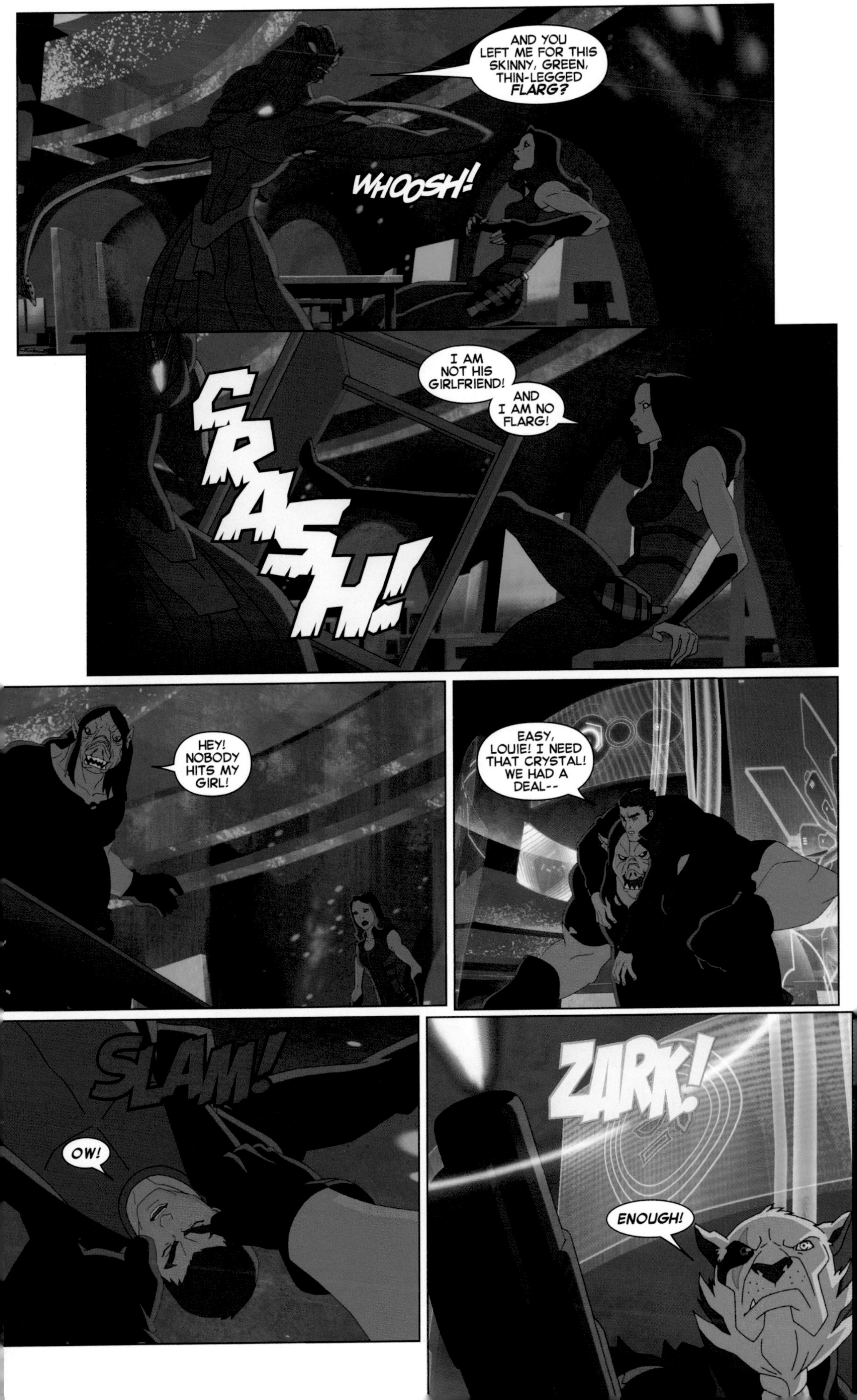
AND YOU LEFT ME FOR THIS SKINNY, GREEN, THIN-LEGGED FLARG?
WHOOSH!
CRASH!
I AM NOT HIS GIRLFRIEND!
AND I AM NO FLARG!
HEY! NOBODY HITS MY GIRL!
EASY, LOUIE! I NEED THAT CRYSTAL! WE HAD A DEAL--
SLAM!
OW!
ZARK!
ENOUGH!

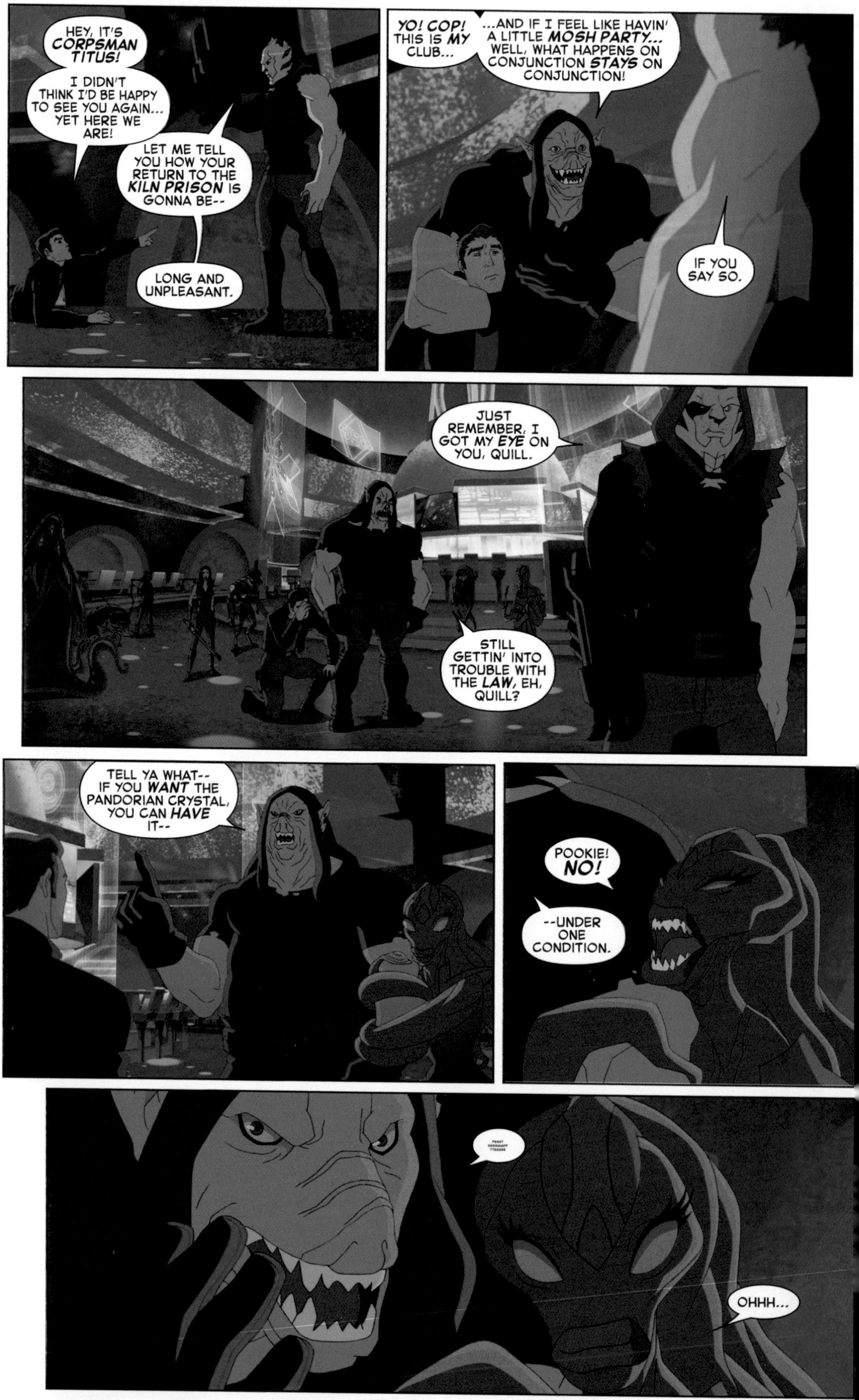
HEY, IT'S CORPSMAN TITUS!
I DIDN'T THINK I'D BE HAPPY TO SEE YOU AGAIN... YET HERE WE ARE!
LET ME TELL YOU HOW YOUR RETURN TO THE KILN PRISON IS GONNA BE--
LONG AND UNPLEASANT.
YO! COP! THIS IS MY CLUB...
...AND IF I FEEL LIKE HAVIN' A LITTLE MOSH PARTY... WELL, WHAT HAPPENS ON CONJUNCTION STAYS ON CONJUNCTION!
IF YOU SAY SO.
JUST REMEMBER, I GOT MY EYE ON YOU, QUILL.
STILL GETTIN' INTO TROUBLE WITH THE LAW, EH, QUILL?
TELL YA WHAT-- IF YOU WANT THE PANDORIAN CRYSTAL, YOU CAN HAVE IT--
POOKIE! NO!
--UNDER ONE CONDITION.
OHHH...

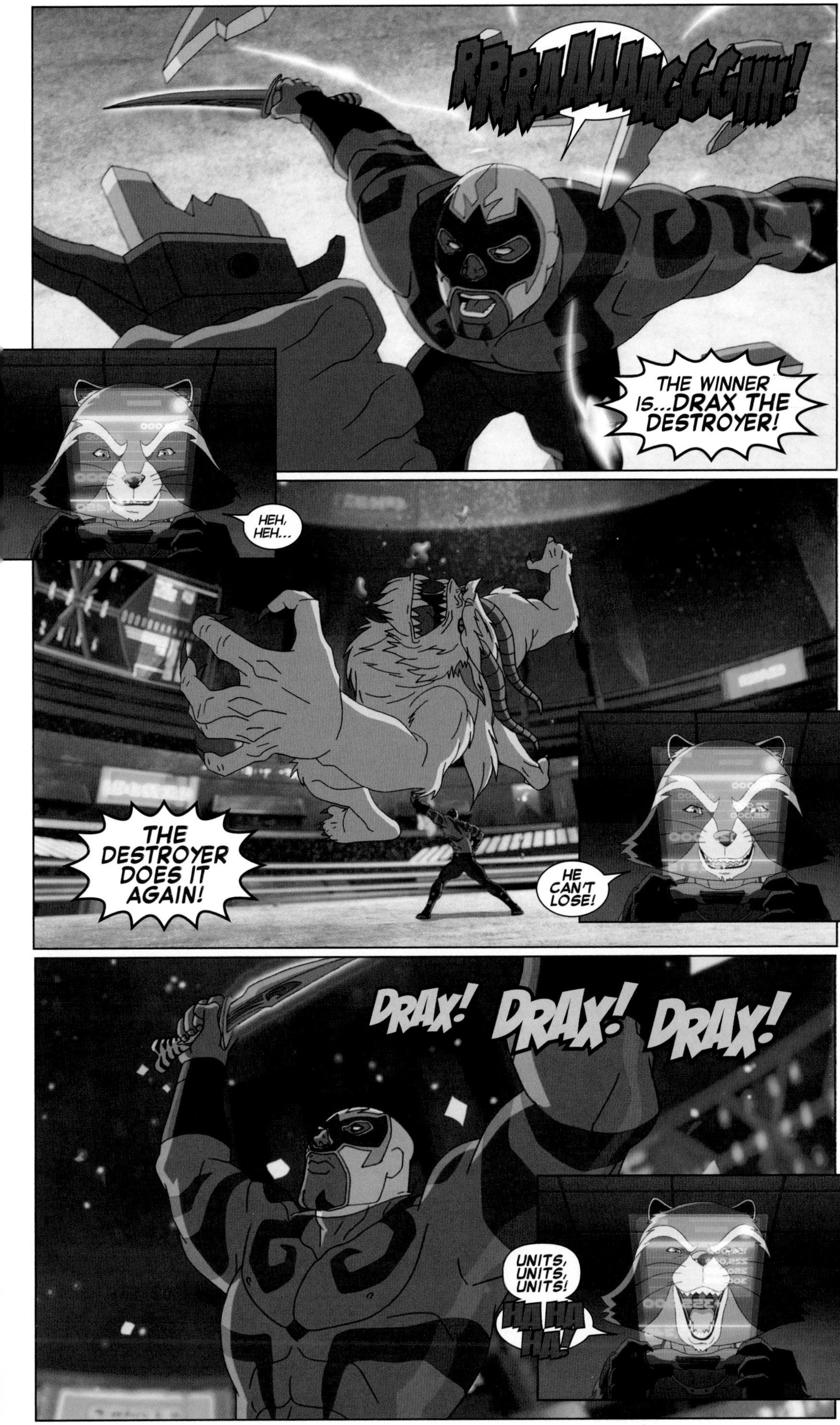
RRRAAAAAGGGHH!
THE WINNER IS...DRAX THE DESTROYER!
HEH, HEH...
THE DESTROYER DOES IT AGAIN!
HE CAN'T LOSE!
DRAX! DRAX! DRAX!
UNITS, UNITS, UNITS!
HA HA HA!

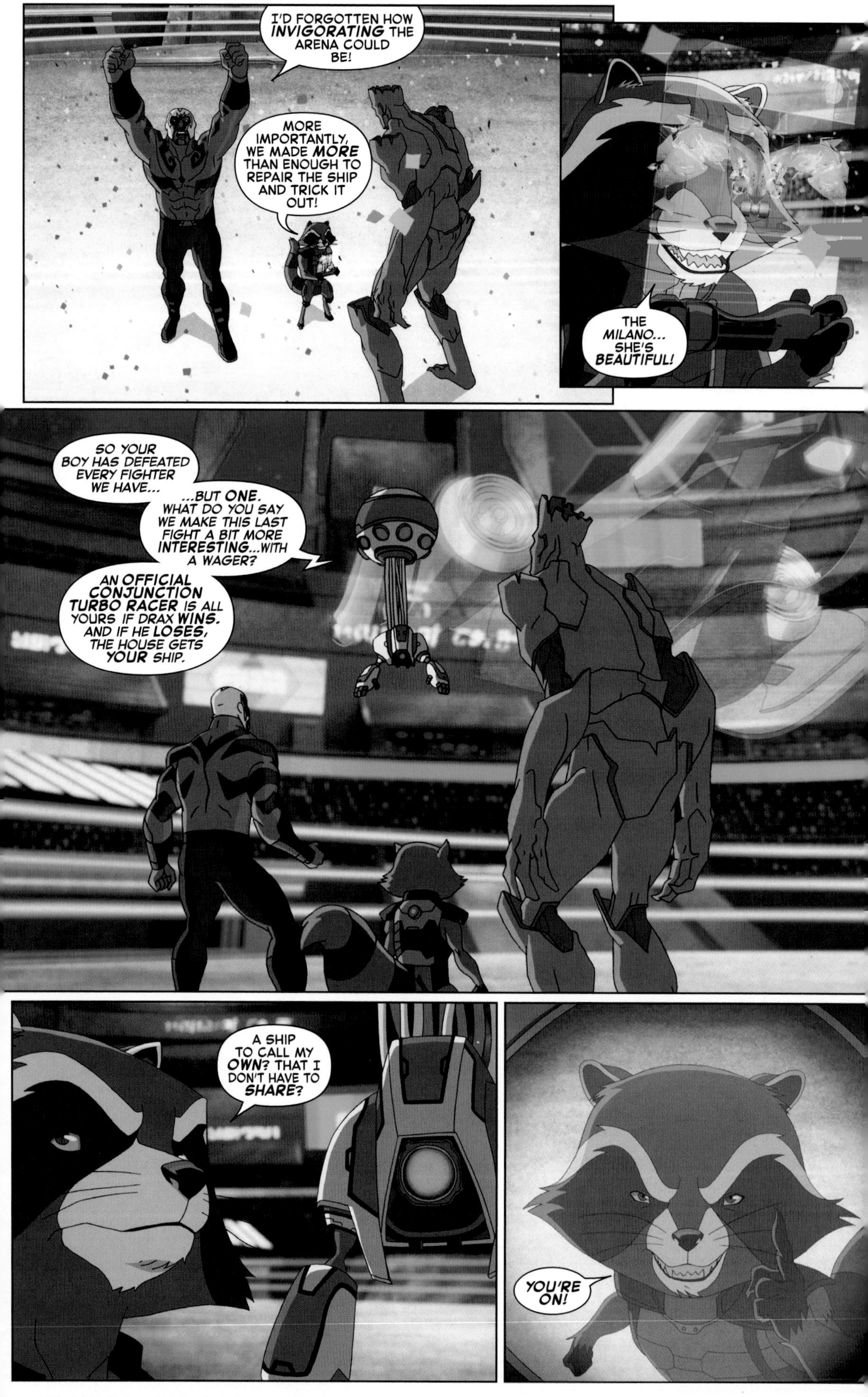
I'D FORGOTTEN HOW INVIGORATING THE ARENA COULD BE!
MORE IMPORTANTLY, WE MADE MORE THAN ENOUGH TO REPAIR THE SHIP AND TRICK IT OUT!
THE MILANO... SHE'S BEAUTIFUL!
SO YOUR BOY HAS DEFEATED EVERY FIGHTER WE HAVE...
...BUT ONE. WHAT DO YOU SAY WE MAKE THIS LAST FIGHT A BIT MORE INTERESTING...WITH A WAGER?
AN OFFICIAL CONJUNCTION TURBO RACER IS ALL YOURS IF DRAX WINS. AND IF HE LOSES, THE HOUSE GETS YOUR SHIP.
A SHIP TO CALL MY OWN? THAT I DON'T HAVE TO SHARE?
YOU'RE ON!

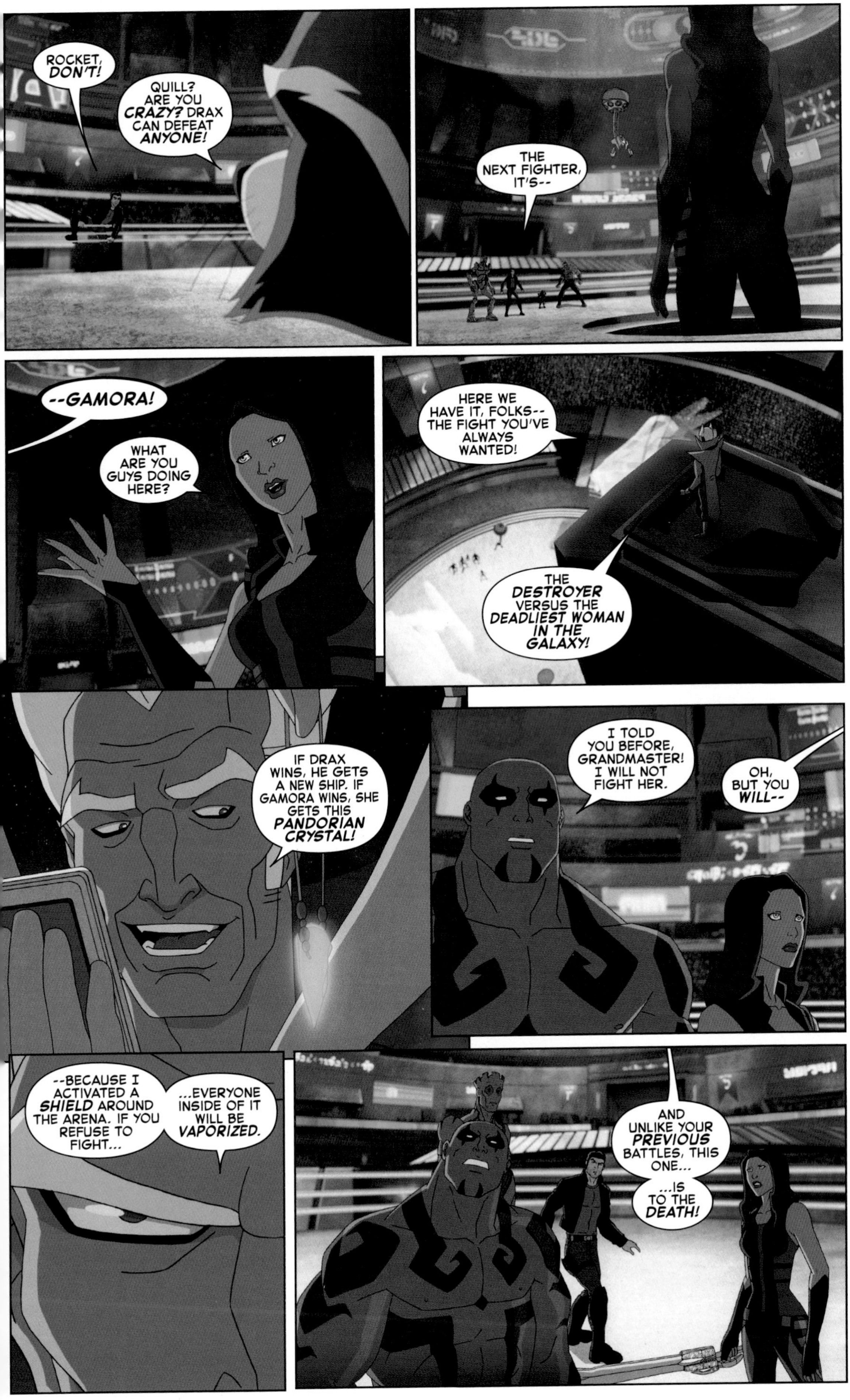
ROCKET, DON'T!
QUILL? ARE YOU CRAZY? DRAX CAN DEFEAT ANYONE!
THE NEXT FIGHTER, IT'S--
--GAMORA!
WHAT ARE YOU GUYS DOING HERE?
HERE WE HAVE IT, FOLKS-- THE FIGHT YOU'VE ALWAYS WANTED!
THE DESTROYER VERSUS THE DEADLIEST WOMAN IN THE GALAXY!
IF DRAX WINS, HE GETS A NEW SHIP. IF GAMORA WINS, SHE GETS THIS PANDORIAN CRYSTAL!
I TOLD YOU BEFORE, GRANDMASTER! I WILL NOT FIGHT HER.
OH, BUT YOU WILL--
--BECAUSE I ACTIVATED A SHIELD AROUND THE ARENA. IF YOU REFUSE TO FIGHT...
...EVERYONE INSIDE OF IT WILL BE VAPORIZED.
AND UNLIKE YOUR PREVIOUS BATTLES, THIS ONE...
...IS TO THE DEATH!

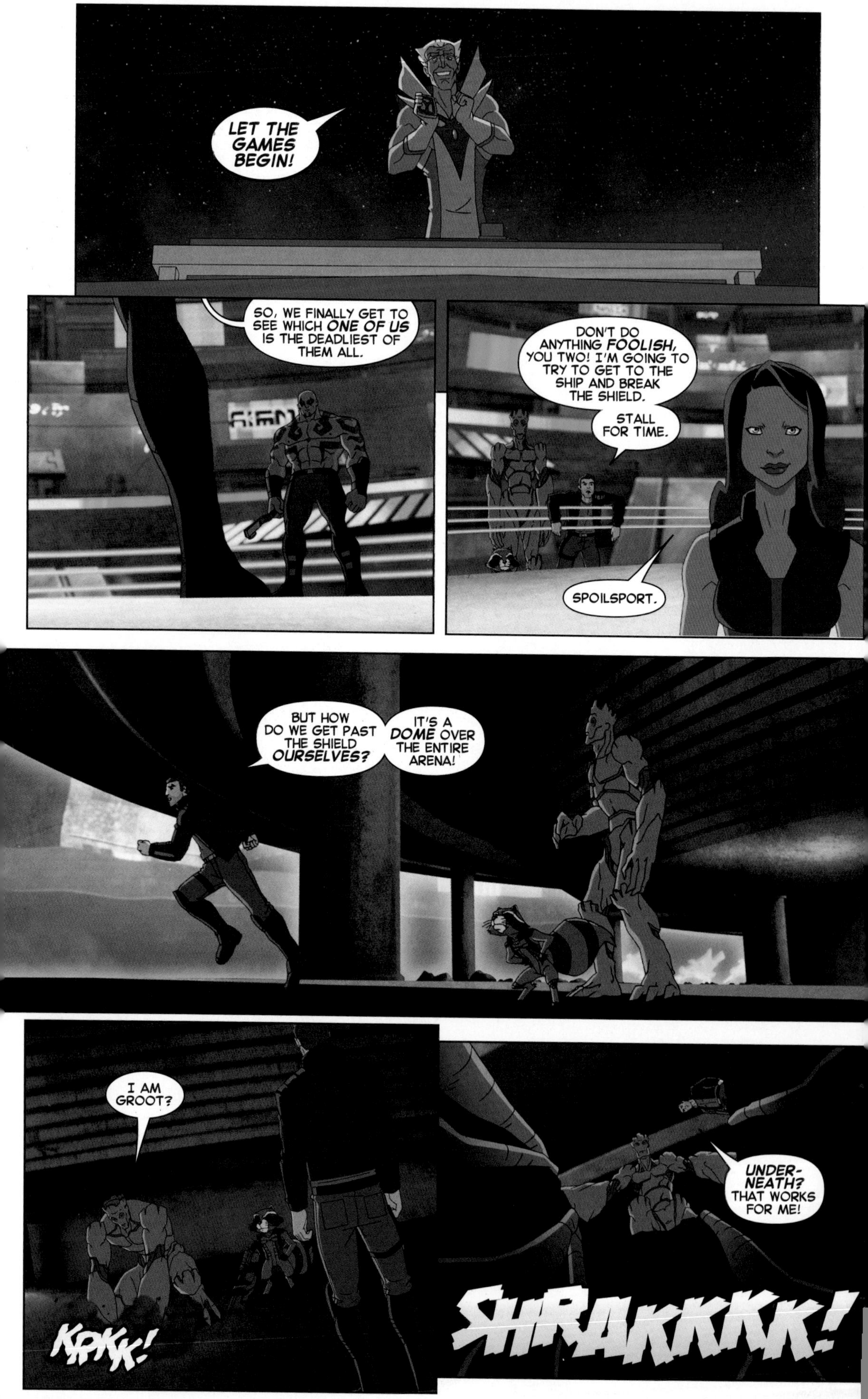
LET THE GAMES BEGIN!
SO, WE FINALLY GET TO SEE WHICH ONE OF US IS THE DEADLIEST OF THEM ALL.
DON'T DO ANYTHING FOOLISH, YOU TWO! I'M GOING TO TRY TO GET TO THE SHIP AND BREAK THE SHIELD.
STALL FOR TIME.
SPOILSPORT.
BUT HOW DO WE GET PAST THE SHIELD OURSELVES?
IT'S A DOME OVER THE ENTIRE ARENA!
I AM GROOT?
KRKK!
UNDER-NEATH? THAT WORKS FOR ME!
SHRAKKKK!

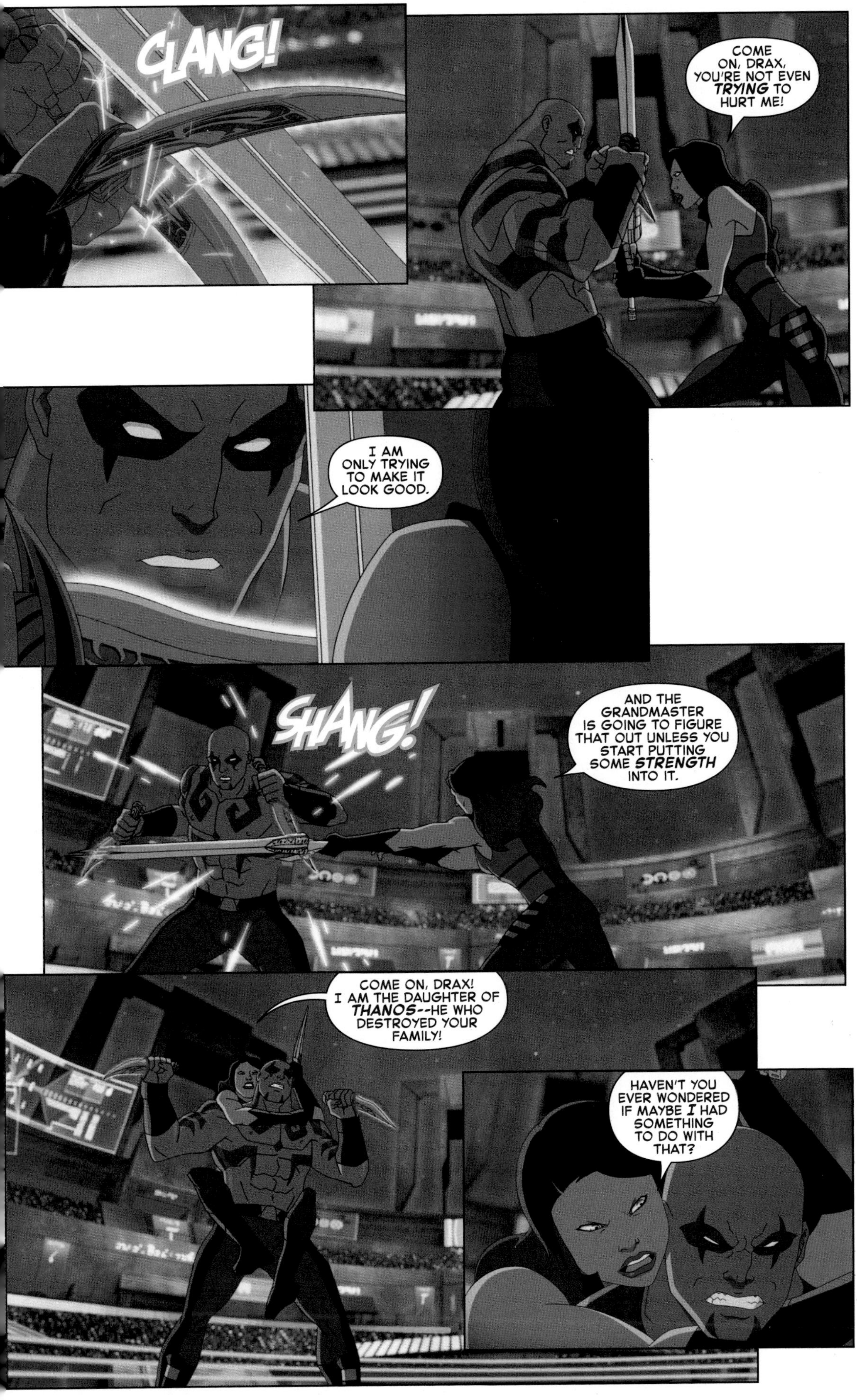
CLANG!
COME ON, DRAX, YOU'RE NOT EVEN TRYING TO HURT ME!
I AM ONLY TRYING TO MAKE IT LOOK GOOD.
SHANG!
AND THE GRANDMASTER IS GOING TO FIGURE THAT OUT UNLESS YOU START PUTTING SOME STRENGTH INTO IT.
COME ON, DRAX! I AM THE DAUGHTER OF THANOS--HE WHO DESTROYED YOUR FAMILY!
HAVEN'T YOU EVER WONDERED IF MAYBE I HAD SOMETHING TO DO WITH THAT?

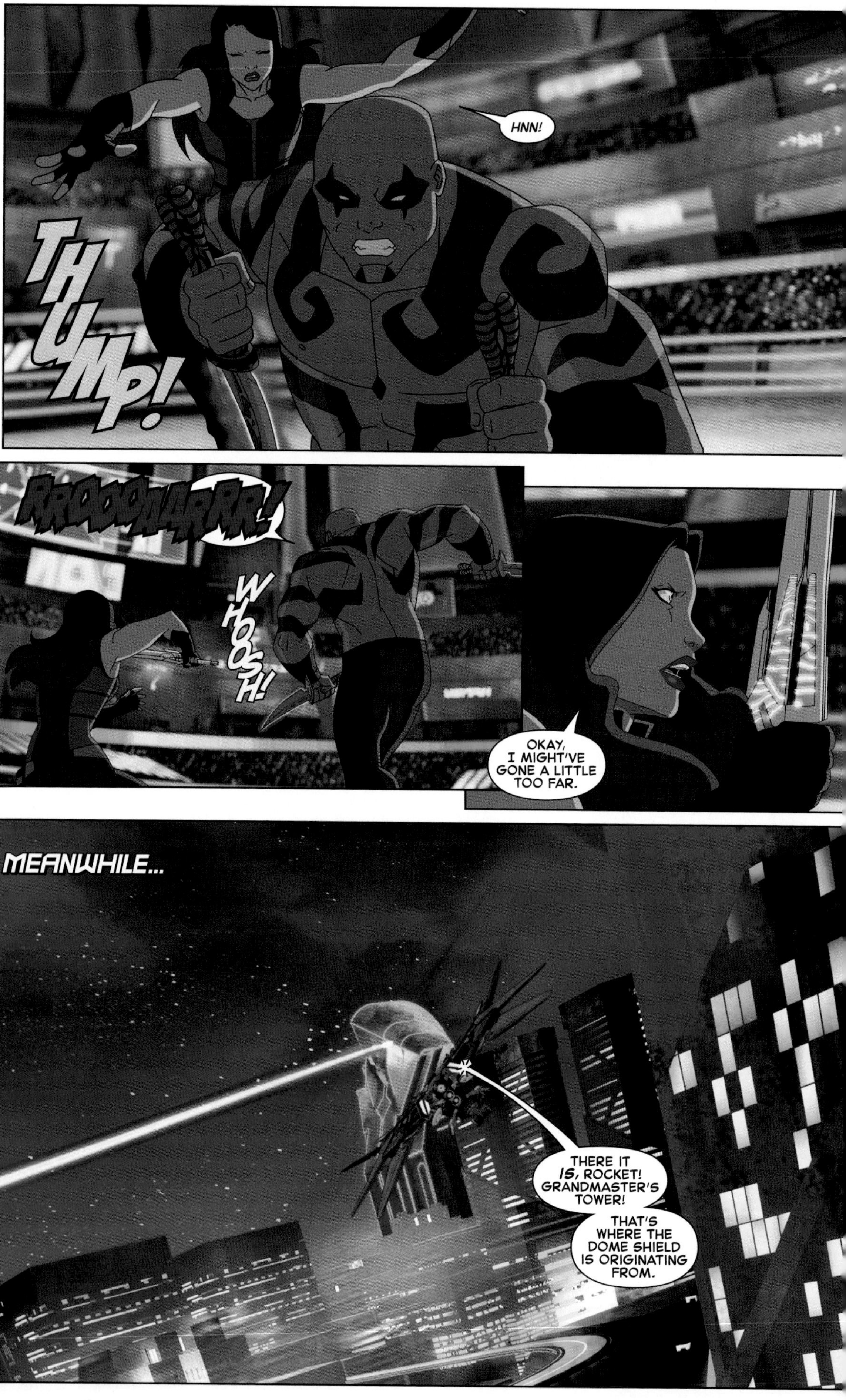
HNN!
THUMP!
RRAOOWARRR!
WHOOSH!
OKAY, I MIGHT'VE GONE A LITTLE TOO FAR.
MEANWHILE...
THERE IT *IS*, ROCKET! GRANDMASTER'S TOWER!
THAT'S WHERE THE DOME SHIELD IS ORIGINATING FROM.

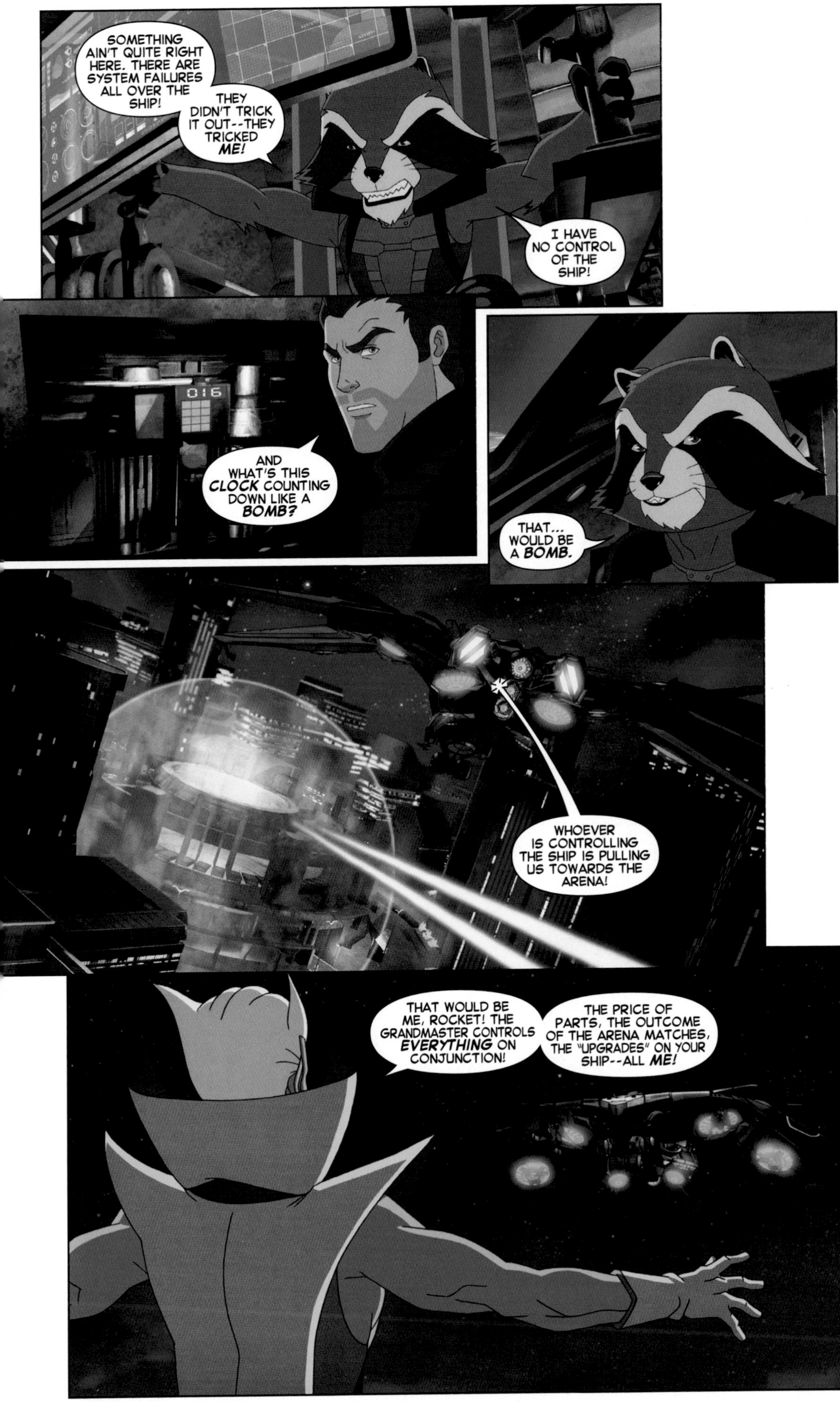
SOMETHING AIN'T QUITE RIGHT HERE. THERE ARE SYSTEM FAILURES ALL OVER THE SHIP!
THEY DIDN'T TRICK IT OUT--THEY TRICKED ME!
I HAVE NO CONTROL OF THE SHIP!
016
AND WHAT'S THIS CLOCK COUNTING DOWN LIKE A BOMB?
THAT... WOULD BE A BOMB.
WHOEVER IS CONTROLLING THE SHIP IS PULLING US TOWARDS THE ARENA!
THAT WOULD BE ME, ROCKET! THE GRANDMASTER CONTROLS EVERYTHING ON CONJUNCTION!
THE PRICE OF PARTS, THE OUTCOME OF THE ARENA MATCHES, THE "UPGRADES" ON YOUR SHIP--ALL ME!

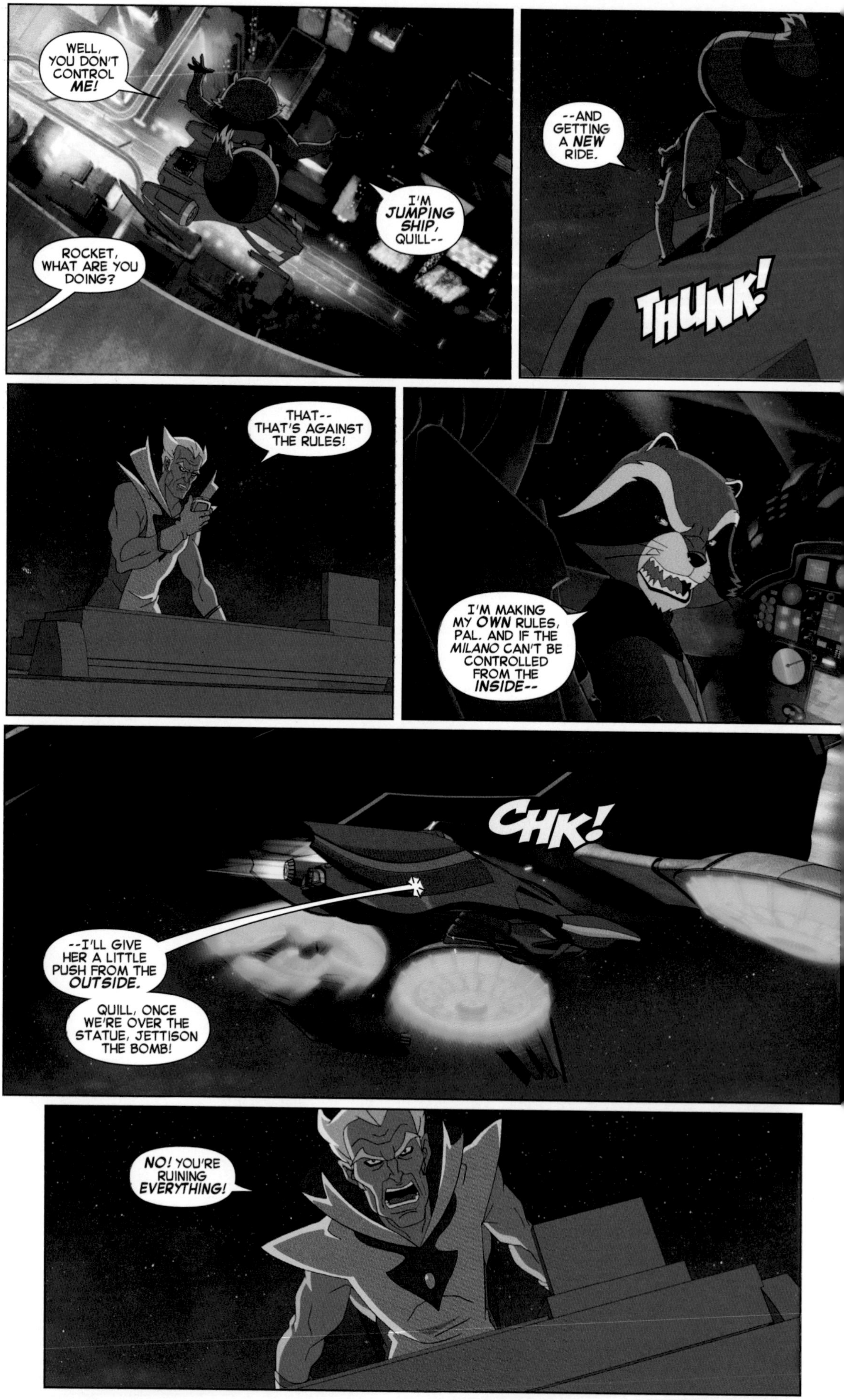
WELL, YOU DON'T CONTROL *ME!*
ROCKET, WHAT ARE YOU DOING?
I'M *JUMPING SHIP,* QUILL--
--AND GETTING A *NEW* RIDE.
THUNK!
THAT-- THAT'S AGAINST THE RULES!
I'M MAKING MY *OWN* RULES, PAL. AND IF THE *MILANO* CAN'T BE CONTROLLED FROM THE *INSIDE--*
CHK!
--I'LL GIVE HER A LITTLE PUSH FROM THE *OUTSIDE.*
QUILL, ONCE WE'RE OVER THE STATUE, JETTISON THE BOMB!
NO! YOU'RE RUINING *EVERYTHING!*

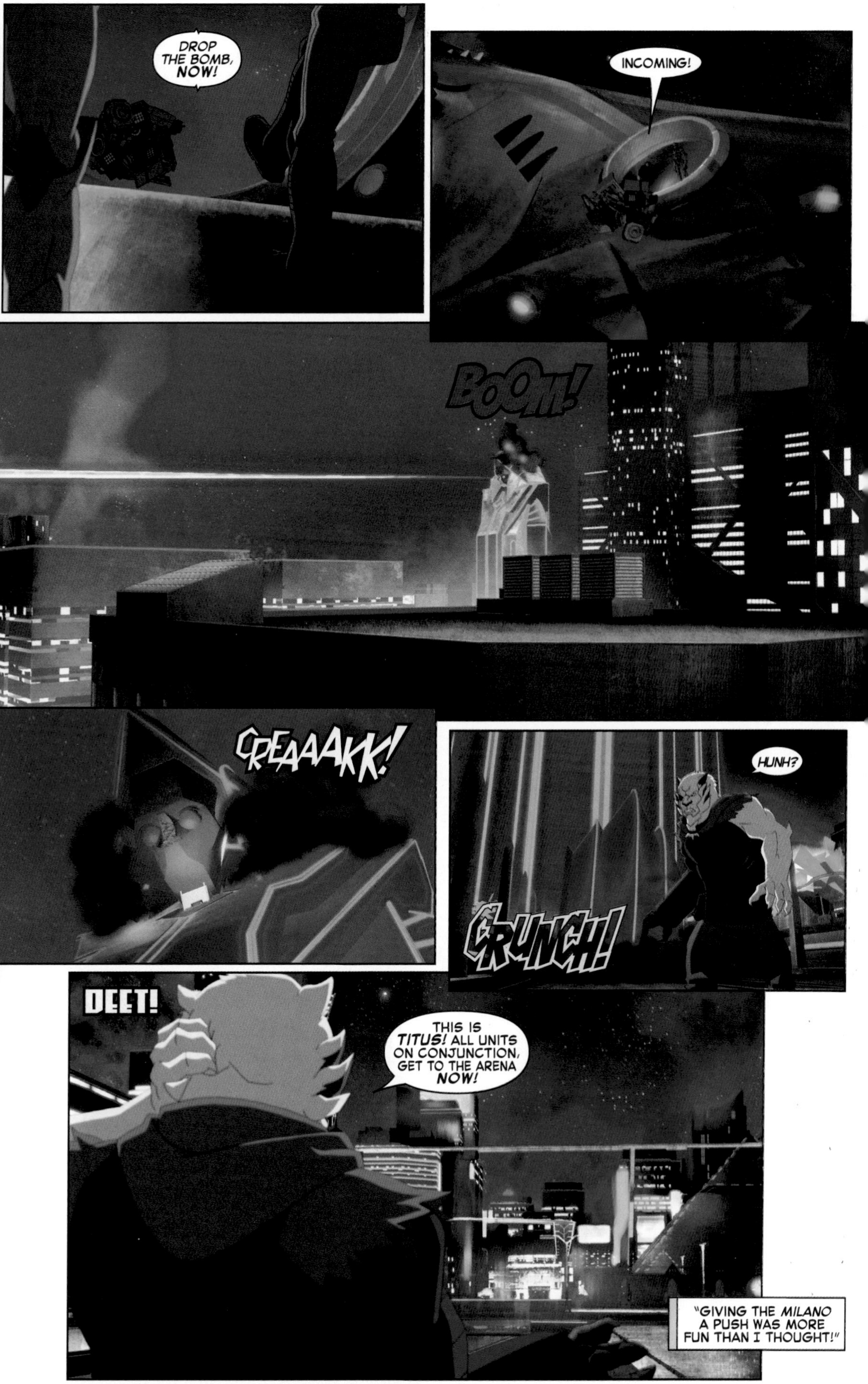
DROP THE BOMB, NOW!
INCOMING!
BOOM!
CREAAAKK!
HUNH?
CRUNCH!
DEET!
THIS IS TITUS! ALL UNITS ON CONJUNCTION, GET TO THE ARENA NOW!
"GIVING THE MILANO A PUSH WAS MORE FUN THAN I THOUGHT!"

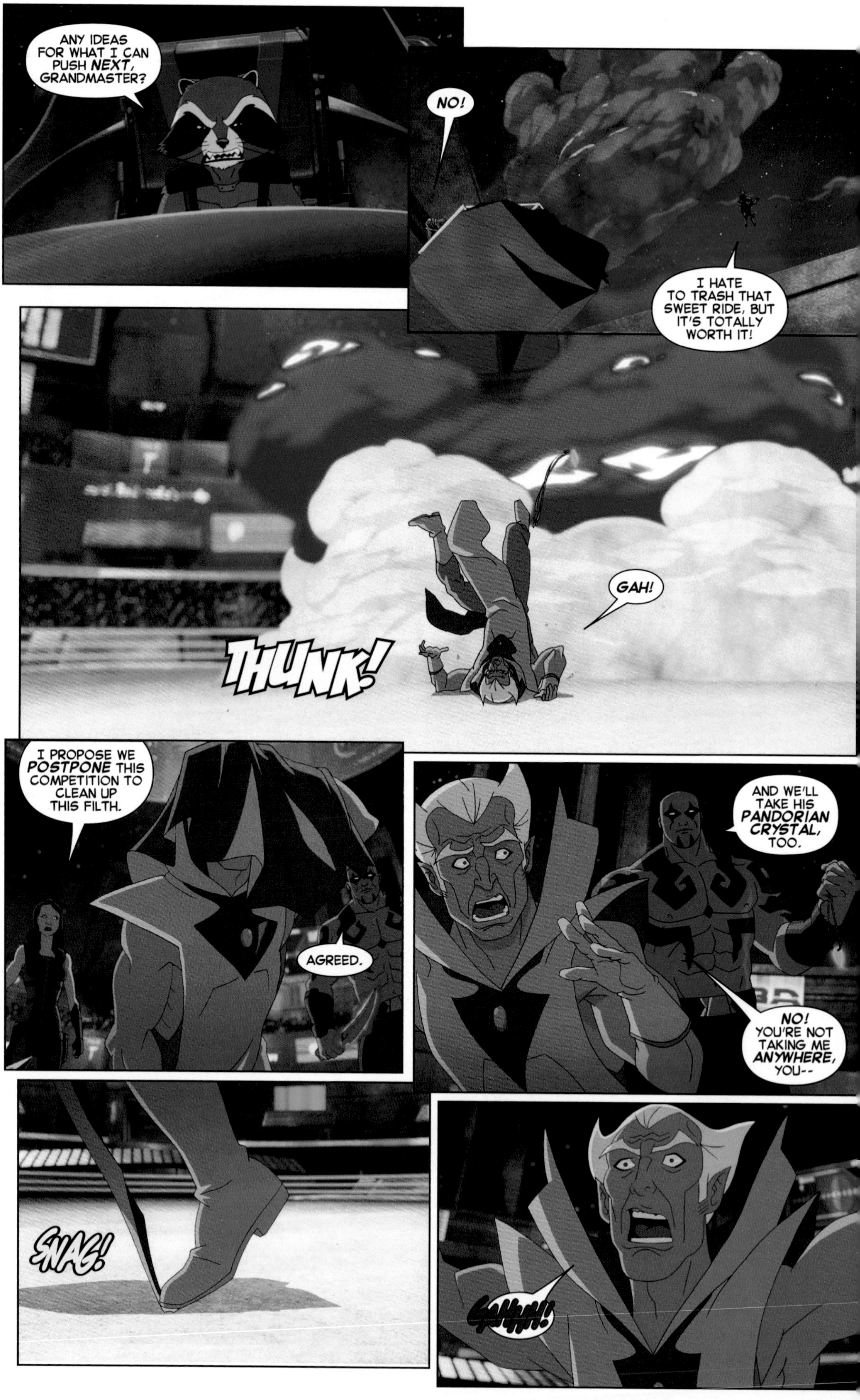
ANY IDEAS FOR WHAT I CAN PUSH NEXT, GRANDMASTER?
NO!
I HATE TO TRASH THAT SWEET RIDE, BUT IT'S TOTALLY WORTH IT!
GAH!
THUNK!
I PROPOSE WE POSTPONE THIS COMPETITION TO CLEAN UP THIS FILTH.
AGREED.
AND WE'LL TAKE HIS PANDORIAN CRYSTAL, TOO.
NO! YOU'RE NOT TAKING ME ANYWHERE, YOU--
SNAG!
GAHHH!

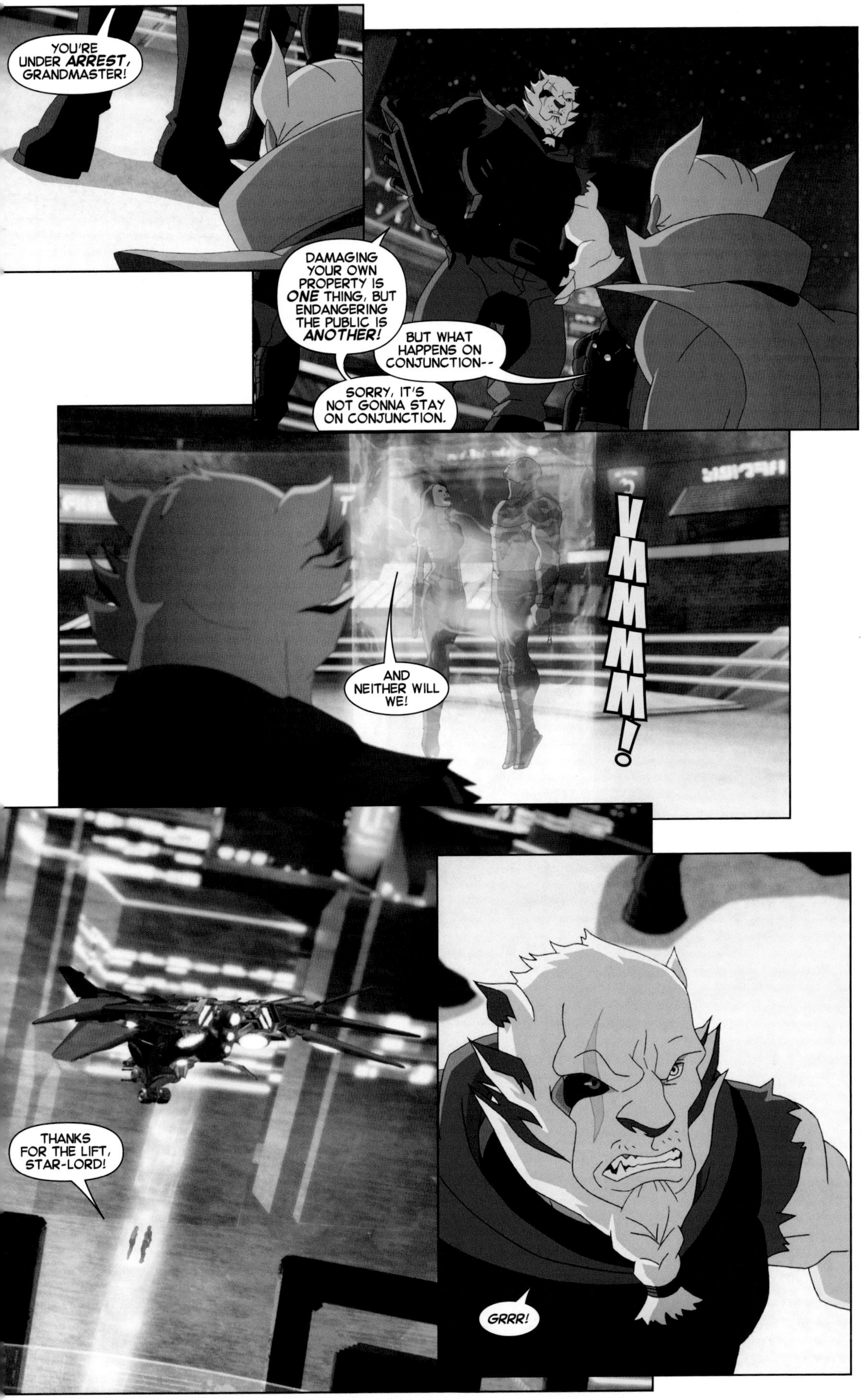
YOU'RE UNDER ARREST, GRANDMASTER!
DAMAGING YOUR OWN PROPERTY IS ONE THING, BUT ENDANGERING THE PUBLIC IS ANOTHER!
BUT WHAT HAPPENS ON CONJUNCTION--
SORRY, IT'S NOT GONNA STAY ON CONJUNCTION.
AND NEITHER WILL WE!
VMMMMM!
THANKS FOR THE LIFT, STAR-LORD!
GRRR!

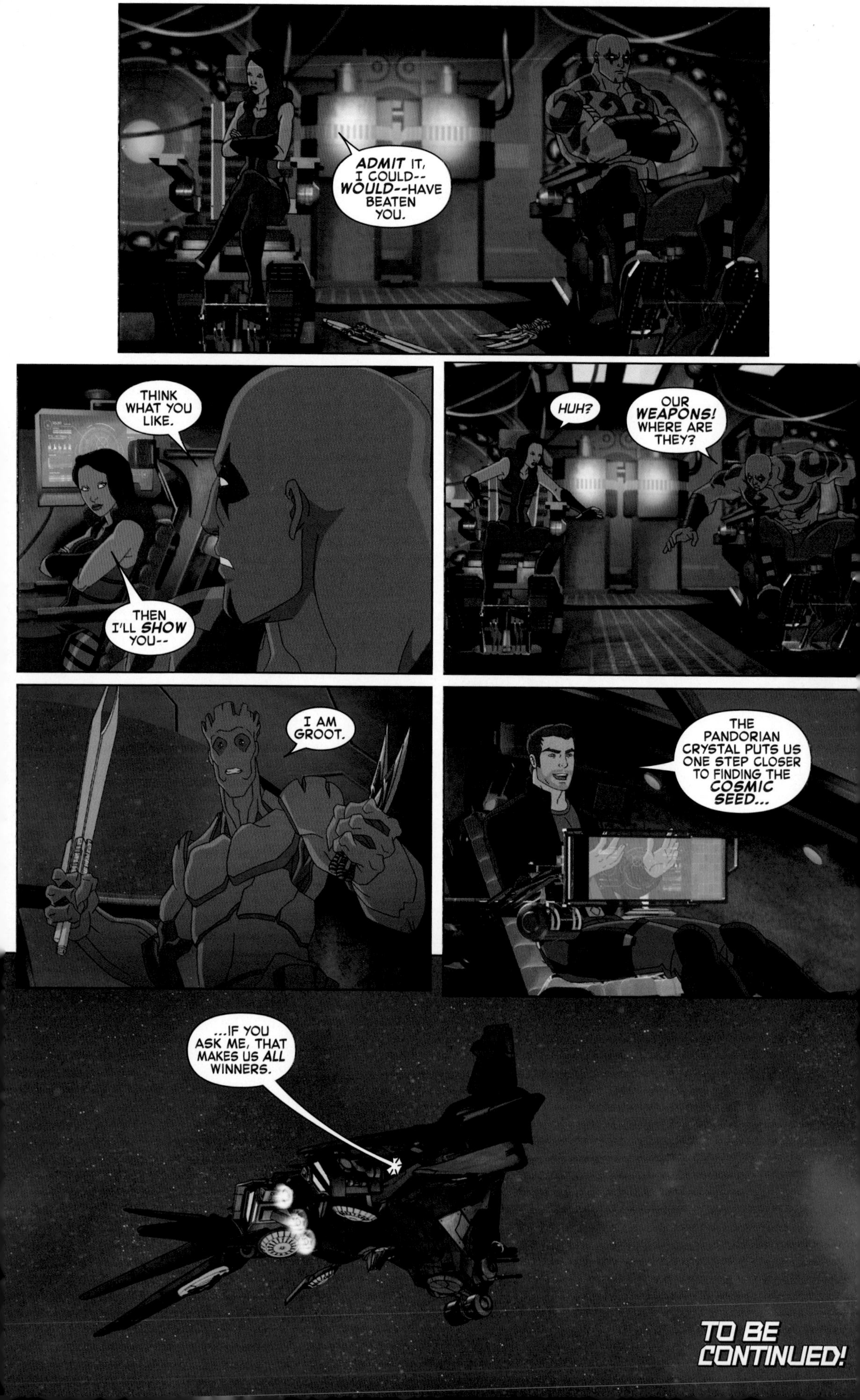
ADMIT IT, I COULD-- WOULD--HAVE BEATEN YOU.
THINK WHAT YOU LIKE.
THEN I'LL SHOW YOU--
HUH?
OUR WEAPONS! WHERE ARE THEY?
I AM GROOT.
THE PANDORIAN CRYSTAL PUTS US ONE STEP CLOSER TO FINDING THE COSMIC SEED...
...IF YOU ASK ME, THAT MAKES US ALL WINNERS.
TO BE CONTINUED!

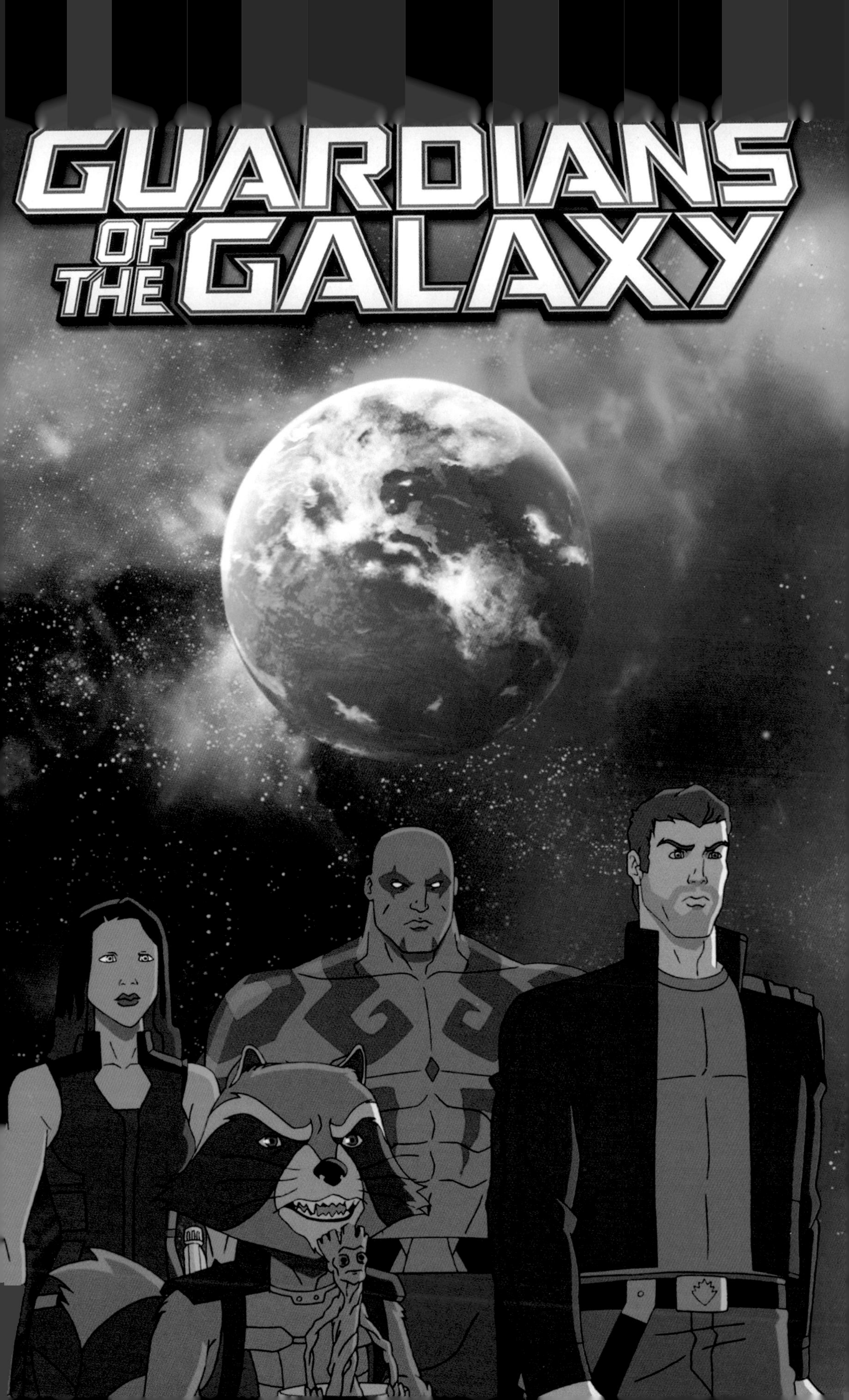
GUARDIANS
OF THE GALAXY

GUARDIANS OF THE GALAXY

COLLECT THEM ALL!

Set of 6 Hardcover Books ISBN: 978-1-5321-4069-3

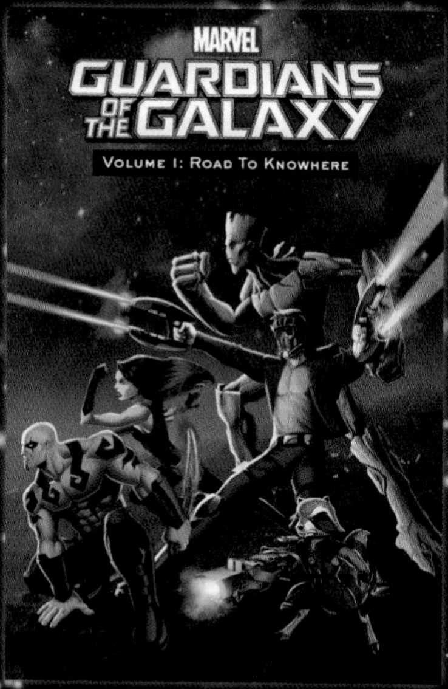

MARVEL
GUARDIANS OF THE GALAXY
VOLUME 1: ROAD TO KNOWHERE

Hardcover Book ISBN
978-1-5321-4070-9

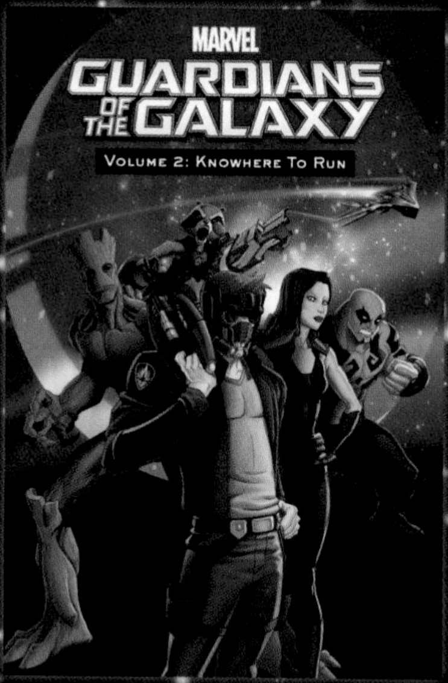

MARVEL
GUARDIANS OF THE GALAXY
VOLUME 2: KNOWHERE TO RUN

Hardcover Book ISBN
978-1-5321-4071-6

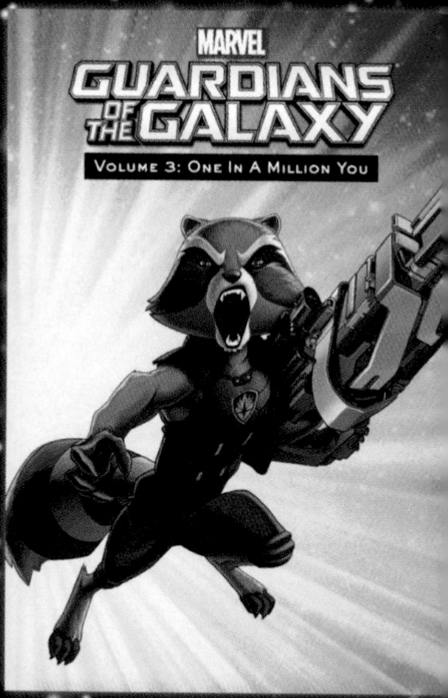

MARVEL
GUARDIANS OF THE GALAXY
VOLUME 3: ONE IN A MILLION YOU

Hardcover Book ISBN
978-1-5321-4072-3

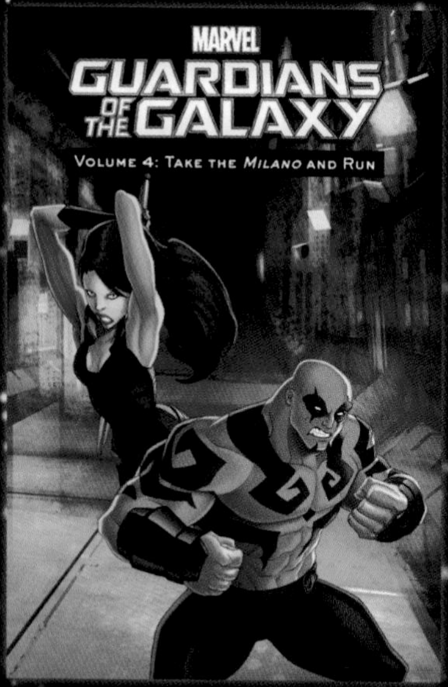

MARVEL
GUARDIANS OF THE GALAXY
VOLUME 4: TAKE THE *MILANO* AND RUN

Hardcover Book ISBN
978-1-5321-4073-0

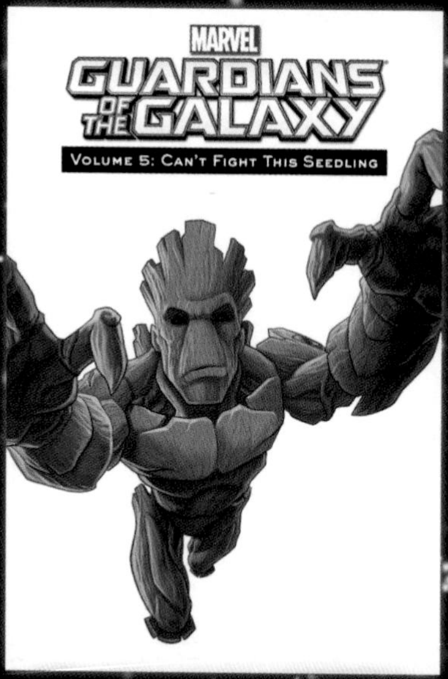

MARVEL
GUARDIANS OF THE GALAXY
VOLUME 5: CAN'T FIGHT THIS SEEDLING

Hardcover Book ISBN
978-1-5321-4074-7

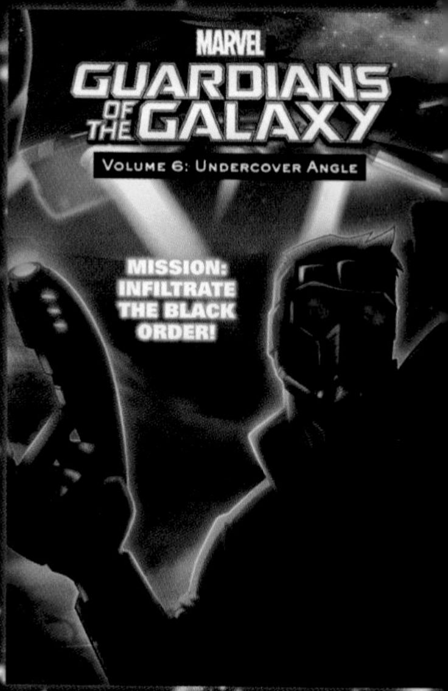

MARVEL
GUARDIANS OF THE GALAXY
VOLUME 6: UNDERCOVER ANGLE
MISSION: INFILTRATE THE BLACK ORDER!

Hardcover Book ISBN
978-1-5321-4075-4